This book is a work of fiction. Any references to historical events, real people, or real locales are used fictitiously. Other names, characters, places, and incidents are the product of the author's imagination, and any resemblance to actual events or locales or persons, living or dead, is entirely coincidental.

SIMON SPOTLIGHT
An imprint of Simon & Schuster Children's Publishing Division
1230 Avenue of the Americas, New York, New York 10020
Copyright © Peyo - 2011 - Licensed through Lafig Belgium -
www.smurf.com All Rights Reserved.
All rights reserved, including the right of reproduction in whole or
in part in any form. SIMON SPOTLIGHT and colophon are registered
trademarks of Simon & Schuster, Inc. For information about special
discounts for bulk purchases, please contact Simon & Schuster
Special Sales at 1-866-506-1949 or business@simonandschuster.com.
Manufactured in the United States of America 1211 CWM
10 9 8 7 6
ISBN 978-1-4424-2291-9

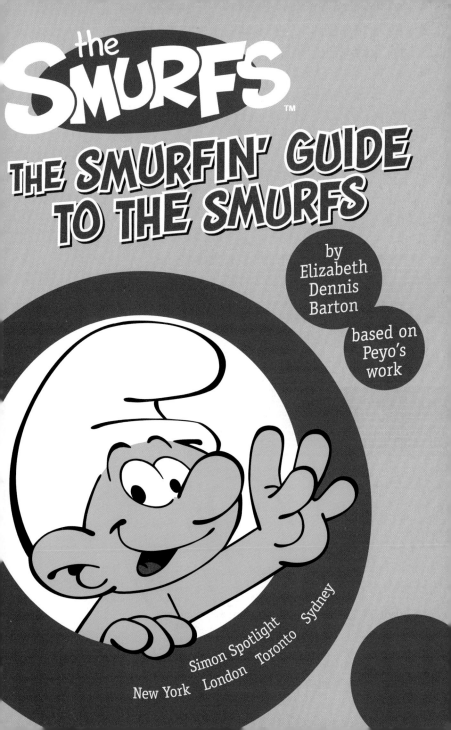

the SMURFS™

THE SMURFIN' GUIDE TO THE SMURFS

by
Elizabeth
Dennis
Barton

based on
Peyo's
work

Simon Spotlight
New York   London   Toronto   Sydney

Contents

Dear Reader,

Today is your smurfy day! Within the pages of this book, you will find everything you need to know about the Smurfs. You are one of the few people Papa Smurf trusts to keep the contents of this book a secret, but before you begin you must smurf the following lines aloud:

"I SOLEMNLY SMURF TO DO EVERYTHING IN MY POWER TO KEEP THIS BOOK SAFE FROM THOSE WHO WISH TO HARM THE SMURFS, SUCH AS PEOPLE NAMED GARGAMEL AND CATS NAMED AZRAEL. FURTHERMORE, I PROMISE TO USE THE SMURFY KNOWLEDGE CONTAINED HEREIN FOR GOOD INSTEAD OF EVIL."

To anyone who breaks this oath, smurf on you! You know what I always say: "Only smurf promises you KNOW you can keep."

Smurfiest wishes,
Brainy Smurf

What the Smurf Is a Smurf?

In a village far, far away, in mushroom-shaped houses, there live tiny creatures called the Smurfs. Smurfs have bright blue skin, speak in a special Smurf language, and only grow to three apples high! They usually wear the traditional Smurf clothing of a white hat and white pants.

You wouldn't know it to look at them, but most of the Smurfs are one hundred years old, and that's not even old for a Smurf! Papa Smurf is 542 years old, and Grandpa Smurf is even older! The Smurfs have a magical object called the Long Life Force Stone that keeps them from getting older. They spend their days trying to keep Smurf Village peaceful and safe.

The Land of the Smurfs

The exact location of Smurf Village is a closely guarded secret. So, more than anything in this book, the map of the Land of the Smurfs is strictly confidential, classified, and just plain hush-hush! In the wrong hands, it will put the Smurfs in grave danger! Now look over your shoulder to make sure no one is watching, and turn the page. . . .

THE LAND OF THE SMURFS

Here it is: the place the Smurfs call home! It is a beautiful land, where sarsaparilla grows wild and the Smurf River flows peacefully. Maybe one day you will see the real thing!

Falls

Smurf Village

Little Bridge

Dam

Windmill

Here is a closer look at the dam, the bridge, and the waterfall that you see on the map. The Smurfs built everything themselves! (Except for the waterfall, of course!)

About one hundred Smurfs live in
Smurf Village, give or take a Smurf. The
village has everything a Smurf needs:
fresh water, fields for growing crops, a
dining hall, and more.

Mushrooms are quite roomy!

Smurfs live in houses that are shaped like mushrooms and painted every color of the rainbow. Here is Handy's house and workshop, Cook Smurf's bakery, and Smurfette's house and garden. Smurfette painted her house in her favorite color: pink! If you lived in a mushroom, what colors would you paint it?

Anatomy
of a Smurf

What do Smurfs look like? Well, they look alike because they wear very similar outfits—usually just a white hat and white pants. Sometimes simpler is smurfier! Of course, some Smurfs wear different clothes. Smurfette wears a white dress and white high heels. Papa Smurf wears red pants and a red hat. And Baby Smurf wears a white onesie (and diapers)!

This kind Smurf offered to be a model of what a typical Smurf looks like:

Hat

Typical Smurf hats look a lot like white knit caps, but with the top part flopping forward. Smurf hats look pretty nice, but they also keep a Smurf's head warm. After all, Smurfs are completely bald until they are very old!

Hands

Smurfs have four fingers on each hand instead of five. Instead of high fives, they give high fours!

Skin

Smurfs have blue skin! But you knew that already.

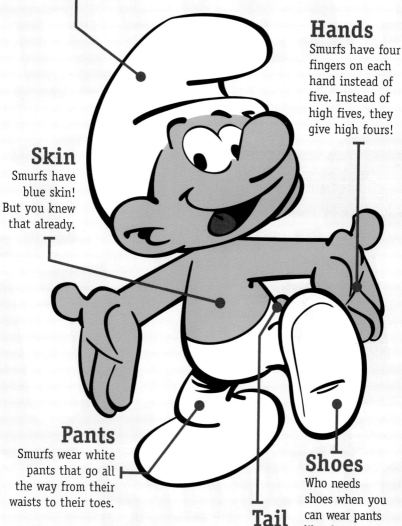

Pants

Smurfs wear white pants that go all the way from their waists to their toes.

Shoes

Who needs shoes when you can wear pants like these?

Tail

Smurfs have little blue tails. They don't serve an exact purpose, but they are very important: The one Smurf who didn't have a tail turned out to be Hogatha in disguise!

And there's more . . .

Since many Smurfs wear the same white outfit, they love to add a little something extra to express their personalities! For example, Brainy Smurf wears glasses because he likes to read, Painter Smurf carries a palette and paintbrush because he likes to paint, and Vanity Smurf wears a flower in his hat because he likes pretty things.

Besmurfed!

Smurf Outfits

If you were a Smurf, what would you wear to help you stand out from everyone else?

For example, if you like to swim, you could wear a cap and goggles, and if you like football, you could wear a helmet.

Your Smurf Outfit

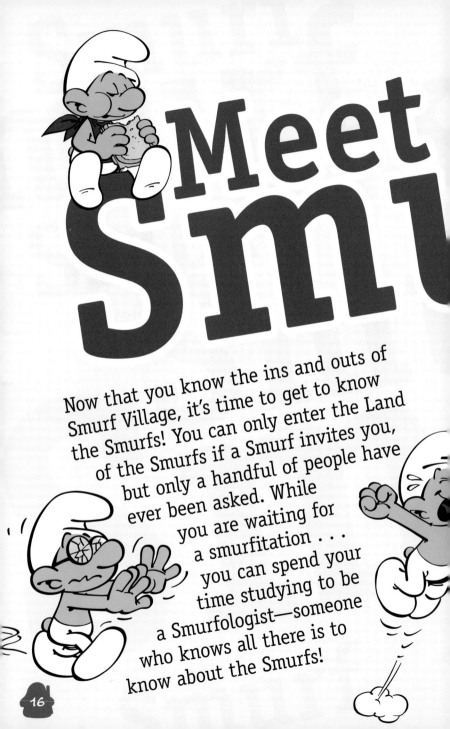

Meet Smu

Now that you know the ins and outs of Smurf Village, it's time to get to know the Smurfs! You can only enter the Land of the Smurfs if a Smurf invites you, but only a handful of people have ever been asked. While you are waiting for a smurfitation . . . you can spend your time studying to be a Smurfologist—someone who knows all there is to know about the Smurfs!

he
rfs!

That's time well-smurfed! Do you know where Smurfette came from or who Clockwork Smurf is? Turn the page to find out the answers to these questions, and a lot more. Let's start with the head honcho. . . .

Papa Smurf

Papa Smurf is the leader of the Smurfs. Unlike the other Smurfs, he has a fluffy white beard and wears red clothes. At 542 years old, he is a wise Smurf and is the one everyone turns to when they need advice. Papa Smurf tries to teach the Smurfs to be kind to one another and to behave like Smurfs instead of like rude humans. In the rare times when humans visit Smurf Village, Papa Smurf treats them with respect and even manages to speak in their language without using the word "smurf." What would the Smurfs do without him?

Papa Smurf tests a growth elixir.

19

This is Papa Smurf's laboratory, where he creates potions to save the Smurfs when they are in danger. The potions don't always work quite right, but it's the thought that counts! If you could ask Papa Smurf to make you a potion, what would you want it to do?

Some of Papa Smurf's favorite potion ingredients are:

nettle juice
salpeter
beads of Helleborus
euphorbia roots

Smurfette

Smurfette was created by Gargamel to lure the Smurfs into a trap. She had wild black hair and spoke with Gargamel through a magic powder compact. After tinkering with some magic potions, Papa Smurf transformed her into the charming Smurfette the Smurfs know and love. All of the Smurfs are in love with her, but she holds a special place in her heart for Poet Smurf.

Smurfette knits a scarf, but it's too long!

23

Brainy Smurf

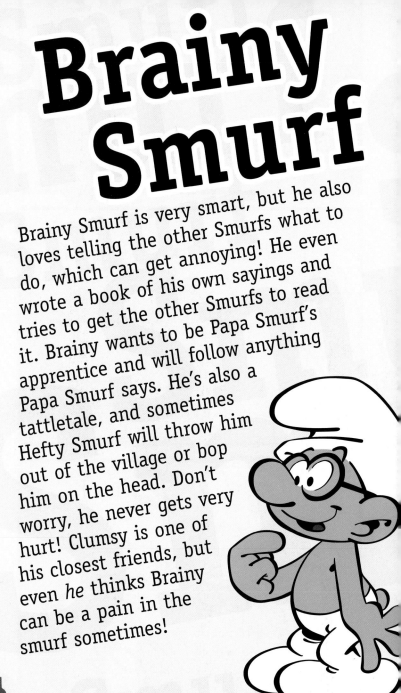

Brainy Smurf is very smart, but he also loves telling the other Smurfs what to do, which can get annoying! He even wrote a book of his own sayings and tries to get the other Smurfs to read it. Brainy wants to be Papa Smurf's apprentice and will follow anything Papa Smurf says. He's also a tattletale, and sometimes Hefty Smurf will throw him out of the village or bop him on the head. Don't worry, he never gets very hurt! Clumsy is one of his closest friends, but even *he* thinks Brainy can be a pain in the smurf sometimes!

"When the only thing Smurfs respect is brawn,
it's tough being the brains of the outfit!"
—Brainy Smurf

Grouchy Smurf

If anyone needs to turn his frown upside down, it's Grouchy Smurf. You can recognize him by his furrowed eyebrows; Grouchy probably even scowls in his sleep! No matter what you say or suggest, Grouchy will be against it. If Astro Smurf says he likes rainbows, Grouchy will say, "Me, I hate rainbows!" If Smurfette says she loves flowers, Grouchy will say, "Me, I hate flowers!" Grouchy has even gone so far as to say, "I hate hate!" From the sound of it, you would think he didn't like anyone or anything, but the Smurfs who know him best know that he has a heart of gold. He just has a bad attitude!

29

Farmer Smurf

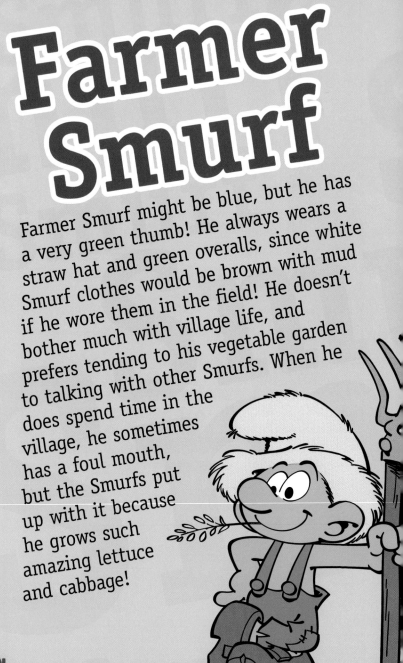

Farmer Smurf might be blue, but he has a very green thumb! He always wears a straw hat and green overalls, since white Smurf clothes would be brown with mud if he wore them in the field! He doesn't bother much with village life, and prefers tending to his vegetable garden to talking with other Smurfs. When he does spend time in the village, he sometimes has a foul mouth, but the Smurfs put up with it because he grows such amazing lettuce and cabbage!

Hefty
Smurf

Hefty by name, and hefty by nature! You can always tell who Hefty Smurf is because he has a heart tattooed on one of his muscular arms. He plays just about every sport you can imagine, and can usually be found in the gym lifting weights. He is someone the Smurfs know they can count on when something difficult has to be done!

Cook Smurf

With his chef's hat and spotless white apron, it's easy to spot Cook Smurf. Near his house you usually can smell delicious warm buns, crusty bread, and every type of cake and tart. The Smurfs absolutely love his food, but Greedy Smurf is his number one fan. Wherever Cook Smurf goes, Greedy is not far behind, ready to snatch a cake or two when Cook Smurf isn't looking!

Handy Smurf

You can recognize Handy by his blue overalls and the red pencil behind his ear. He is always ready to get to work. Not only can he fix anything, he also has invented 1,001 useful machines: a robot, a plane, a train, and even a machine that can smurf blue skies when it's raining. He's always ready to build a house or a bridge or a contraption to trap Gargamel, all at a moment's notice! He's just so handy!

Harmony Smurf

As a true music fan, Harmony just loves to play any instrument he can find. Unfortunately, the only sounds he can get out of them are often deafening QUAAACKS and SCREEEEECHES—to the horror of his companions. Even a music box plays out of key when he gets hold of one!

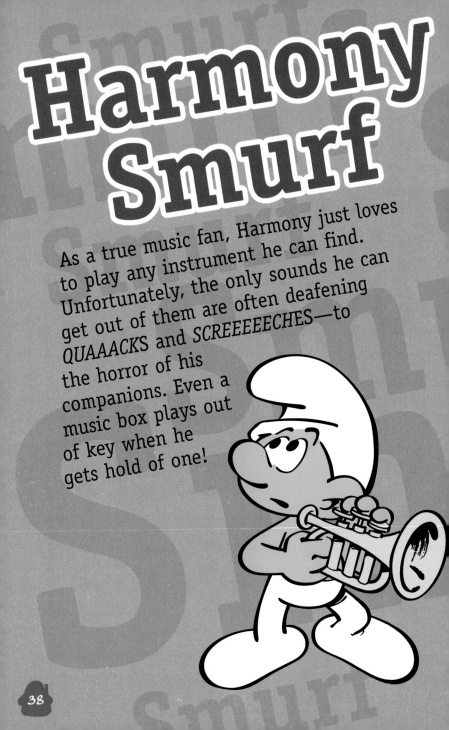

Vanity Smurf

With a flower in his hat and a mirror in his hand, Vanity is the Smurf who cares the most about how he looks. Delicate and sensitive, he spends his time talking about fabrics with Smurfette and admiring his reflection in the mirror. If his mirror breaks, he is the unhappiest Smurf in the world.

45

Painter Smurf

Painter Smurf lives only for his art. His brushes, paints, and canvasses are his most treasured possessions. He turns them into landscapes, portraits, and still lifes. Needless to say, Smurfette is one of his favorite models. Sometimes, though, the other Smurfs can't tell who or what is the subject of his paintings. Don't they know he's an *artiste*?

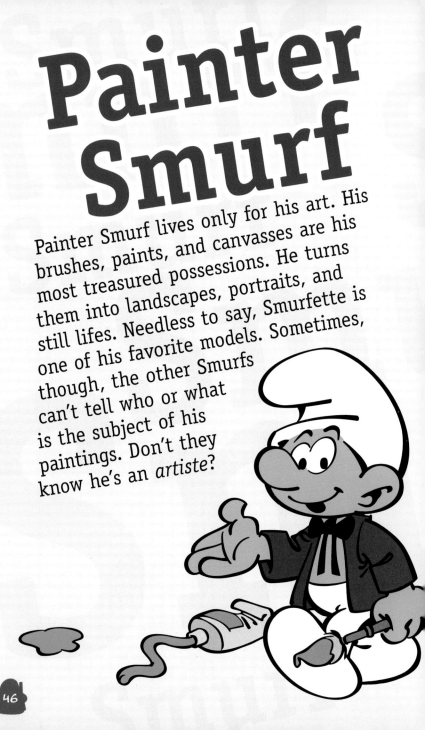

47

Clumsy Smurf

Nobody wants Clumsy's help because they know that whatever he does, it never ends well! Even when he simply picks up a hammer, all the other Smurfs run away because they are afraid of being hit on the head. Poor Clumsy!

Wild Smurf

Wild Smurf is the only Smurf with the courage to stand up to Gargamel. He doesn't know the meaning of the word "fear." Brought up from a young age by some friendly squirrels after being lost as a baby, Wild Smurf just cannot get used to village life and smurfy habits. He lives in the forest and wears a Smurf hat made of woven leaves.

King Smurf

When Papa Smurf left the village to collect ingredients for a potion, Brainy proclaimed himself "King Smurf." He dressed in gold clothing and a red cloak, put on a crown, and carried a mushroom scepter. Then he forced the Smurfs to build him a castle and dig a moat around the village. He also put Jokey in jail for giving him an exploding gift! When Papa Smurf returned and was very angry, King Smurf apologized. He let the Smurfs turn his royal outfit into a scarecrow for Farmer Smurf's fields—and went back to being Brainy Smurf again.

Smurflings

Most of the Smurfs are one hundred years old, but the four Smurflings are younger and smaller than the other Smurfs. Slouchy, Nat, and Snappy Smurfling used to be regular Smurfs. One day they were trapped in Father Time's backward-running grandfather clock and became young Smurflings again. Then they wanted Smurfette to have a friend to play with so they created a girl Smurfling, named Sassette, from a block of clay. The Smurflings are only two apples tall, but they have big personalities: Nat loves animals and nature, Slouchy is laid-back, Sassette is a tomboy, and Snappy has a bad temper.

Nat

Nature "Nat" Smurfling lives up to his name. He is a great friend to all animals and a protector of the Earth. He never goes anywhere without his pet caterpillar. He often wanders around the forest with Wild Smurf and loves every minute of his time outdoors.

Snappy

Snappy likes to think of himself as the leader of the Smurflings. He wears a shirt with a thundercloud on the front because he has a bad temper and snaps at the other Smurflings when he doesn't get his way. He also gets angry when he thinks the Smurfs are giving him advice just because they're older than him.

Slouchy

It is easy to mix up Slouchy with Lazy Smurf. But unlike Lazy, Slouchy is not a slacker, and he doesn't fall asleep when he's supposed to be helping Farmer Smurf. Slouchy is simply laid-back. His motto is "smurf and let smurf"; he doesn't bother anybody and expects others to not bother him either.

Sassette

Sassette was created from a block of blue clay just like Smurfette. Sassette has red hair and freckles, wears overalls, and says things like "jumpin' jackrabbits" and "chatterin' chipmunks," and calls Papa Smurf "Pappy"! She is a tomboy at heart, and while she prefers to play with the boys, she and Smurfette think of each other as sisters and want the best for each other.

54

Miner Smurf

Miner Smurf spends his time at the bottom of mines digging, digging, and digging. But what exactly is he digging for? Gold? Diamonds? Not at all, because, like all the other Smurfs, he doesn't care about making a profit. He's digging for iron, copper, lead, and all sorts of other things that may be useful to the Smurfs, but especially for Handy.

Grandpa Smurf

A long time ago, when Papa Smurf was still a young Smurf, Grandpa Smurf was the leader of the village. Then he left on a journey to find more fuel for the Long Life Force Stone in the mountains. He and Nanny Smurf are retired, and they live in a remote area in the mountains.

Nanny Smurf

Nanny Smurf lives with Grandpa Smurf in the mountains. From time to time they venture back down to the village to say hi to the Smurfs. The Smurfs love the visits as much as they love Nanny Smurf's cookies, which is saying a lot!

Purple Smurfs

Purple Smurfs can't be trusted. As soon as a Smurf turns his back—*snap!*—the Purple Smurf will bite his tail. Then the regular Smurf will turn purple, grit his teeth, and hop around Smurf Village trying to bite another Smurf's tail. Luckily, Papa Smurf has a cure for Purple Smurf bites: Pollen from a tuberose flower makes Purple Smurfs sneeze and turns them back into regular Smurfs. *Phew!*

Clockwork Smurf

Handy created Clockwork Smurf because he needed help with all of the tasks in Smurf Village. With Clockwork Smurf around to lend a hand, Handy can do what he loves even more than being handy: inventing! The Smurfs accept Clockwork Smurf *almost* as if he were a real Smurf.

59

Reporter Smurf

Reporter Smurf is a Smurf who believes in telling the truth at all times. He started his newspaper to put an end to all the gossip in Smurf Village, and he tries to not take sides when he writes. To Reporter Smurf, the Smurfs will be a lot smurfier if they read the news!

Tailor Smurf

Tailor Smurf loves to sew, and he loves patterns and colorful fabric! He makes all of the Smurfs' clothing, and tries to get them to try new looks, but most Smurfs just want to wear their standard white pants and white hats. Poor Tailor Smurf! At least he can make dresses for Smurfette!

Smurf Friends Forever

The Smurfs aren't the only ones in the forest. Here are some of their smurfiest friends!

Johan and Peewit

Johan is a teenage knight who rides around his kingdom on a white horse. He often travels with his friend Peewit, a young jester who rides a goat. Johan is usually very polite and has good manners. He is good at sword fighting and archery, and is very courageous. Peewit sings and plays the mandolin, but not very well! However, he is always there to help his friend Johan when danger calls. With the help of Homnibus, an enchanter and a close friend of Papa Smurf's, Johan and Peewit were able to visit the Smurfs.

Puppy

Puppy is a friendly dog who was given to Papa Smurf as a gift. But Puppy obeys no one but Baby Smurf, who is the only one who can open the locket around Puppy's neck. They can often be seen running from one side of the village to the other, Baby Smurf hanging on to Puppy's furry back and giggling away!

Besmurfed!
Smurf Names

Smurfs are usually named after things they like to do or the way they act. Grouchy Smurf is always cranky and Painter Smurf likes to paint and draw. If you were a Smurf, what would your name be?

Your Smurf Name

The Anti

Not everyone is smurfy with the Smurfs. Here are some of the Smurfs' main enemies, starting with you-know-who. . . .

Smurfs & Gargamel

For someone who really hates the Smurfs, Gargamel sure spends a lot of time trying to find them! He is an evil wizard and lives in his cottage with a mangy cat named Azrael. The first time Gargamel ever saw a Smurf was when he was in wizard school. Azrael captured Brainy Smurf, and Gargamel knew that Smurfs were the missing ingredient in the potion that turns regular metal into gold. Luckily, Papa Smurf rescued Brainy, but Gargamel has always sworn to capture the Smurfs. Fortunately for the Smurfs, Gargamel isn't so smart, and so far they have always found a way to escape.

Gargamel's
Workshop

This is Gargamel's workshop, where he makes all of his evil potions. These are some of Gargamel's favorite ingredients:

drool of toad
stinkbug spit
eye of newt
slug slime
pond scum
rhinoceros earwax
root of mandragora
rattlesnake venom
snow leopard hair balls

This flea-bitten cat is Gargamel's sidekick. He follows the wizard everywhere, hoping his master will one day catch a tasty little Smurf and throw it to him to eat. That hasn't happened yet. But even though he is as stupid as Gargamel, he is a threat to any Smurfs who wander close to Gargamel's hut.

Scruple

Scruple is a boy who was kicked out of wizard school for being a troublemaker and sent to work as his uncle Gargamel's apprentice. Whenever Scruple has a good idea, Gargamel pretends he thought of it . . . but Scruple gets the last laugh because he usually can see the holes in Gargamel's plans. He calls his uncle "Gargie" to make him angry.

How to Speak Smurf

The Smurf language is one of the easiest to learn—most of the words are the same as in English! Just replace some nouns, verbs, and adjectives with the word "smurf" and you'll be speaking smurfily in no time. The catch is, one phrase can mean many things, so don't get discouraged if you don't *always* understand what the Smurfs are saying.

A few key Smurfisms are:

Run for your lives = *Run for your smurfs*
Where's the bathroom? = *Where's the smurfroom?*
I love you = *I smurf you*
Best friends forever = *Best smurfs forever*
It's a beautiful day = *It's a smurfy day*
What time is it? = *What smurf is it?*
Good morning = *Good smurfing*
Sweet dreams = *Smurf dreams*
That's great = *That's smurfy*
Absolutely right = *Absosmurfly right*
Piece of cake = *Piece of smurf*
Happy birthday = *Happy Smurf Day*
Happily ever after = *Smurfily ever after*
Fa██ous = *Smurfulous*
Magnificent = *Smurfnificent*
Fantastic = *Smurftastic*
Awesome = *Smurfsome*
Lucky = *Smurfy*
Pretty = *Smurfy*
Happy = *Smurfy*
Hungry = *Smurfy*

Papa Smurf's

Words of Wisdom

"Giving you a bath, Baby Smurf, makes me about as wet as taking one myself."

Papa Smurf: Grouchy, it is my smurfological opinion that you will stay sick unless you cheer up!

Grouchy: I *hate* cheering up!

"Ah, success! Sometimes it takes a lot of work, and many failures, before an experiment finally Smurfs!"

"All for Smurf, and Smurf for all!"

"You're only as old as you think you are, if you think at all; if you Smurf as young as you think you are, you'll feel ten feet tall."

"Enough fighting! Let's all have a smurfy day!"

Brainy Smurf: Is it much further, Papa Smurf?

Papa Smurf: Not much further, my little Smurfs.

Jokey Smurf [later]: Is it much further Papa Smurf?

Papa Smurf: Not much further, my little Smurfs.

Grouchy Smurf [even later]: Is it much further, Papa Smurf?

Papa Smurf: Yes, it is!

I'm Hungry!
What Is There to Smurf? (Smurf Food)

Smurfberries

The Smurfs' main source of nutrition is the smurfberry! Smurfberries are round red or blue berries that grow on a bush. Smurfberry bushes only grow in the Smurf forest and on a remote island in the middle of the ocean that is guarded by a sea witch. The Smurfs drink smurfberry juice and use the fruit to make smurfberry pies and other desserts. Mmm, smurfy!

Sarsaparilla

Smurfs love sarsaparilla leaves almost as much as they love smurfberries.

Nuts

Smurfs also eat nuts like chestnuts, acorns, and walnuts. In the fall they gather nuts to eat during the long winter.

Cook Smurf's
Recipe for Smurfy Smurfberry Muffins

There's nothing like one of Cook Smurf's famous Smurfy Smurfberry Muffins in the morning. Just ask Greedy Smurf! Whenever they are baking, Greedy runs straight to the bakery to get some fresh out of the oven. Cook Smurf usually makes a double batch of muffins: one for Greedy, and one for everyone else! Wasn't it nice of him to share the recipe? **Don't forget to ask a grown-up for help!** You'll have your own Smurfy Smurfberry Muffins in no time!

Makes about 30 Smurf-size muffins!

Ingredients:
- 2 cups all-purpose flour
- 3 teaspoons baking powder
- 1/2 teaspoon salt
- 3/4 cup granulated sugar, plus 1/4 cup for topping
- 1 egg
- 1 cup milk
- 1/4 cup vegetable oil
- 1-1/3 cup fresh smurfberries
- blue food coloring
- cooking spray to grease mini-muffin pans

Directions:
1. Preheat oven to 400 degrees Fahrenheit.
2. In a large bowl, combine the flour, baking powder, salt, and 3/4 cup sugar.
3. In a small bowl, beat the egg. Then add the milk and oil. Pour into a well in the flour mixture.
4. Mix gently with a fork until it forms a batter.
5. Add blue food coloring until the batter looks *really* smurfy (about 30 drops).
6. Mix in one cup of fresh smurfberries.
7. Spray mini-muffin pans with cooking spray.
8. Spoon batter into mini-muffin cups.
9. Sprinkle 1/4 cup sugar on top of muffins.
10. Bake for 14 minutes, or until golden (and blue).

A note from Cook Smurf:
If you can't find smurfberries in your local supermarket, you can substitute blueberries or raspberries.

Jokey Smurf's Smurfiest Jokes

Jokey is known for exploding "gifts," but he also likes telling jokes. Here are some of his most smurftastic!

Painter Smurf: Blue looks really good on you, Smurfette. You should wear it every day!
Smurfette: I do!

Question: What would you call a Smurf who likes to go to the beach?
Answer: Surf Smurf!

Question: Why did one Smurf ask another Smurf if he was cold?
Answer: Because he was all blue!

Question: What did Lazy Smurf say to the bumblebee?
Answer: Buzzzzzzzzzzzzzz . . . (Not much before he fell asleep!)

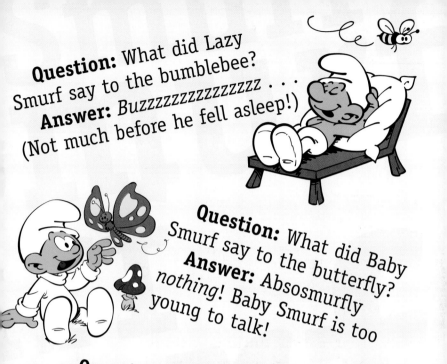

Question: What did Baby Smurf say to the butterfly?
Answer: Absosmurfly nothing! Baby Smurf is too young to talk!

Question: Which room do Smurfs eat smurfberry porridge in?
Answer: The Mush Room!

Question: What are Greedy Smurf's favorite words?
Answer: More, more, and

What Do Smurfs

They go swimming and diving:

Smurf for Fun?

They wrestle:

They ski:

They ice-skate:

They box:

Smurfs also love to travel for fun! To go long distances, they usually ride on the back of a stork. These giant birds are their friends, and thanks to them, the Smurfs are able to visit faraway lands. They also travel by stork to keep an eye on Gargamel.

Maybe one day you will stumble upon Smurf Village, or the Smurfs will visit you. Until then, we present you with this Certificate of Smurfhood, making you an honorary Smurf!

I, Papa Smurf, upon the recommendation of Brainy Smurf proudly smurf to you,

_____,

your name here

also known as

_____,

your Smurf name here

this *Certificate of Smurfhood* on this most smurfy day, _____.

today's date

Papa Smurf

PAPA APPROVED